The Clever Cat

Eleanor Frances Lattimore

with illustrations by the author

The Clever Cat

Eleanor Frances Lattimore

with illustrations by the author

SECOND EDITION

FRANKLIN COUNTY LIBRARY
906 N. MAIN ST.
LOUISBURG, NC 27549
BRANCHES IN BUNN,
FRANKLINTON, AND YOUNGSVILLE

ISBN-13: 978-0692636350 (Indigo Hill Books)
ISBN-10: 0692636358

Indigo Hill Books
Louisburg, North Carolina
United States of America

Contents

1

ULYSSES, THE CAT

THERE was once a cat named Ulysses. He lived in a white house in a town in New Hampshire, where the winters are long and snowy and the summers are short but very pleasant. It was a good thing that the house was white; because Ulysses was black, and when he sat on the doorstep he could be seen from a long way off and looked very important.

Ulysses was a big cat. He was black all over except for a white spot under his chin like a white necktie. His fur was as smooth and shiny as a sea lion's, and his eyes were as big and round as an owl's eyes, and green.

Nobody knew where Ulysses came from or where he had lived when he was a kitten. Maybe he didn't know himself. He came to the white house one cold winter night, when there was frost on his whiskers and snow on his back; and he tapped on the front door with his paw.

When the door was opened he ran inside the house just as though he belonged there. He went straight to the kitchen and sat in front of the stove, and as soon as he was given some food he ate and ate as though he hadn't eaten for a long time.

When he had eaten all that was good for him he was put down in the cellar so that he could get warm in front of the furnace. And there he curled up and went to sleep in a wheelbarrow.

The family who lived in this house liked cats. They hoped that Ulysses would stay with them, but they were afraid he might go away as suddenly as he had come. He might be a wandering cat, they thought, who never liked to stay in any place for very long. So they named him "Ulysses" after a famous wanderer. But when the next day came, Ulysses wouldn't even go outdoors.

He stayed in the white house and became the family's cat. And soon it seemed as though he had always lived there.

2

THE HOUSE AND THE FAMILY

ULYSSES liked having a home. He liked having a name, too. "Ulysses" was a good name, he thought. It sounded much better than "kitty."

There were two grown-up people in the family, and two children. Ulysses soon learned that the two grown-ups were named "Father" and "Mother," because that was what the children called them.

The children were named Judith and Rose. Judith, who was seven years old, had long brown hair that was usually braided in two braids; and Rose, who was six years old, had short yellow hair that curled all over the top of her head. They both had brown eyes, and they were both very lively.

Although Ulysses didn't like to go outdoors and freeze his paws in the snow, he found lots of things to do in the nice, warm house. He started to explore right away.

First, there was the cellar. The cellar was a pleasant place, because the furnace kept it warm, and the red wheelbarrow that was kept there made a good bed for a cat. The cellar was also an exciting place. There was a dark corner where coal was stored, and a closet where there were baskets full of potatoes and apples.

There were all kinds of tools in the cellar, too; hammers, and rakes, and spades, that sometimes fell over when they were bumped into.

Then there was the kitchen. The kitchen was a sunny room with green curtains at the windows and green and white checked linoleum on the floor.

The stove was there, of course, and the refrigerator, and it was a good room for a cat to be in. Ulysses soon knew on just which shelf in the refrigerator the canned cat food was kept, and when he was hungry he tried to claw open the refrigerator door.

Next to the kitchen was the dining room. There was a big table there that Ulysses was not allowed to jump on. There was a sideboard, too, that Ulysses was not allowed to walk on. He didn't have much fun in the dining room except when there was nobody around in the room but himself.

The living room, though, across the hall, was a fine room for a cat. All the most comfortable chairs were there, and he could take naps in them. There was a fireplace in the living room, with a rug in front of it. Ulysses liked to sit on the rug and watch the fire and feel warm all over.

Upstairs were the bedrooms. That meant more places where Ulysses could take naps, and more corners for him to explore. There was a doll's house in the children's room just big enough for him to get inside. And there were closets and shelves and desks upstairs, and a sewing-machine and a laundry basket.

The doll's house was just big enough for Ulysses to get inside.

There was so much to see and to explore in the house that Ulysses didn't have time for many naps, at first. He liked to be upstairs and he liked to be downstairs, and he didn't know which he liked better. Perhaps that was why he spent so much time pattering up and down the stairs.

Up and down he went, in a great hurry, looking as though he were the busiest and most important cat in the world.

But the times when Ulysses felt sure he was the happiest cat in the world were in the evenings, when Father and Mother and Judith and Rose were all together in the living room, sitting around the fire, and he was there too. Then he tucked his paws under him, and purred. Because, although he was glad that he had a house to live in, he was even happier that he had a family.

3

AN ENEMY

IT WAS sad for Ulysses when he had to go out of doors. Father said he must go out for some fresh air every day, just as the children did. Ulysses wouldn't go out by himself, though. Father had to open the door and give him a gentle push from behind. When the door was shut Ulysses sat on the doorstep with his ears back. He hunched himself into a furry black ball and looked and felt very cold.

One winter day Ulysses was sitting hunched up on the doorstep. He had been outdoors only a little while, but it seemed like a long time to him. He didn't want to move very far away from the door because he was hoping that someone would open it soon and let him into the warm house again.

Ulysses was thinking of the fire in the fireplace in the living –room, and of the rug in front of it that was half red and half gray. When Ulysses lay on the rug he lay half on the red side and half on the gray side. Red and gray were very becoming to his black fur, everyone said.

Rose and Judith were playing out of doors. They didn't seem to mind the cold. They had on green leather ski-suits, and woolen caps and mittens.

Judith and Rose were learning how to ski.

Rose and Judith were learning how to ski. They had long skis strapped to their boots and they each had two ski-poles. They pushed themselves along with their poles, and slid on their skis across the hard snow that shone like a white frosted cake. Sometimes their skis went faster than they did. When this happened, Judith and Rose sat down hard.

Ulysses watched the children. Rose had just sat down hard, and Judith was having trouble with her skis, which had run into each other and became crossed, so that she couldn't move.

"Oh, dear!" said Judith. "My toes are crossed!"

Ulysses unwrapped his tail from around his legs, and stretched. Then he bounded away across the snow. It looked as though he were running to help Judith.

Before he reached her, though, he stopped short. His back arched and his tail bristled. Coming towards him from the house across the street was something very black and very fierce-looking.

It was a long time since Ulysses had seen another cat. He had probably seen many in his kitten-days, but he had almost forgotten what they looked like. This black thing coming towards him was really only another black cat, but Ulysses thought it was an enemy.

"Miaow! Psst!" he said.

It didn't take long for the other cat to answer him. "Miaow! Psst!" he replied, and flew at Ulysses. There was a whirl of snow, and a waving of bristling tails.

Father heard a twig crackle in the nearest tree. He looked up and there was Ulysses!

Over and around the two cats rolled in the snow, till you couldn't tell which was which; and Judith and Rose, who watched the fight, were afraid they were going to eat each other up like the Gingham Dog and the Calico Cat. They could only cry, "Oh!"

But the fight was over as quickly as it had begun. The whirling black ball turned into two cats, one running in one direction and one in another. They each ran up a tree, where they sat twitching their tails. So Rose and Judith went on with their skiing.

Jimmy, the little boy next door, came out with his skis to join them. And they all went off down the road together, seeing who could ski the fastest.

A little later Father opened the front door and called Ulysses. He was surprised not to find him right outside waiting to come in. He heard a twig crackle in the nearest tree, and looked up. There was Ulysses!

Ulysses looked a little foolish when he saw Father. He settled down more comfortably on his branch and tried to look as though he had just climbed up there to admire the view. When Father called him again he climbed down the tree trunk slowly and trotted across to the front door, as quietly and peacefully as though he had never been in a fight. Father was not fooled, though. He had seen the chewed spot on Ulysses' left ear.

When Ulysses was lying on the rug in front of the fire, half on the red and half on the gray, he heard Father say to Mother, "Ulysses was in a fight today. Look at his ear! I think he must have been fighting Blackie."

Ulysses cocked his other ear and opened one eye. "Blackie," he thought. "So that's what his name is! Well, I like 'Ulysses' better." And he closed his eye again and went to sleep.

But after that day Ulysses liked going out of doors even less than he had before, because he knew that he would find his enemy waiting for him outside. It isn't much fun to have your ear chewed.

4

A TRIP TO THE ATTIC

ULYSSES had lived in the white house for some time before he discovered the attic. He had been up and downstairs hundreds of times and thought he knew every corner of the whole house. But he didn't know there was an attic; and he had never noticed a chain that hung down from a trap door in the upstairs hall. That was because it was so high above his head.

No one went into the attic much in the winter, as it was cold up there. But one day Ulysses heard a rattling sound, and then a sliding sound, that he had never heard before. He was so startled that he hid under Judith's bed. What had happened was that Father had pulled the chain that let down the trap door, and then pulled down the attic stairs.

Ulysses waited under the bed, and listened to the sound of footsteps going up and up, as though someone were climbing to the roof. He was so curious that he came out of his hiding place to see what was happening.

There in the upstairs hall were some new stairs that he had never seen before! They stood perfectly still, so Ulysses put one paw on the lowest step. It didn't move, so he put another paw on the next step. In another moment he had bounded up the stairs, and there he was in the attic. His eyes were as round, and his whiskers were as excited-looking as though he had just done something very dangerous.

Ulysses put one paw on the lowest step. It didn't move, so he put another paw on the next step. In another moment he had bounded up the stairs.

And certainly the attic was a dark and dangerous place. Huge trunks were there, making dark shadows; and there were piles of suitcases and cardboard boxes and wrapping paper. The walls slanted together on both sides and met, like the top of a tent, so that there was no ceiling. There were no windows either except for a small one like a half moon at the end.

Father was in the attic, looking among the cardboard boxes for one that was good and strong, because he had some things that he wanted to mail. He was stepping on a piece of wrapping paper which made a rustling sound, so that he didn't hear Ulysses coming up the stairs. As soon as Ulysses saw that Father was there he felt quite safe. He started off to explore.

How exciting the attic was! Behind the suitcases and trunks the slanting walls made long, dark tunnels. Ulysses walked all around the trunks and suitcases and down the dark tunnels, stepping softly on his padded feet.

In a far corner Ulysses found some toys that Judith and Rose had grown tired of.

In a far corner he found some toys that Judith and Rose had grown tired of. Mother had put them away for a while, thinking that Judith and Rose might like to play with them again sometime on a rainy day. There was a Noah's Ark, a rocking horse, a box of mixed up crayons, and a doll's cradle with no doll in it.

Ulysses sniffed at the crayons to see if they were good to eat, rubbed up against the legs of the rocking horse, and chewed the string that was fastened to the Noah's Ark. Then he lumped inside the doll's cradle to see if it was the right size for him. And it was just the right size.

Ulysses was tired of exploring, so he thought he would rest for a while. He curled his tail around his hind legs, and his paws around his nose.

Meanwhile Father had found the kind of box he wanted. Down the attic stairs he went, and when he stepped off the last stair he turned around and pushed the stairs up. He only needed to give one push, before the stairs slid up easily. The door in the ceiling closed, and the upstairs hall looked just as usual.

No one knew that Ulysses was in the attic, and no one missed him until dinner time, three hours later. Then Father said, "I wonder where the cat is?" And mother called, "here, puss, here, puss!"

There was a dish of cat food waiting for him under the kitchen table. But no cat appeared. Judith and Rose slid down from their chairs at the same time, laying their napkins on the table. "May we go look for Ulysses?" they asked.

"Yes," said Mother. "But don't be too long or your dinner will get cold. He is probably upstairs asleep on one of the beds."

Judith and Rose ran through the house hunting for Ulysses. He wasn't upstairs and he wasn't downstairs. He wasn't in the cellar either.

They went to the front door and called, "Here, puss puss puss!" But there was no cat outdoors except Blackie, who was either going for a walk or looking for his enemy.

Judith shut the door. "Where *can* Ulysses be?" she said.

"I know one place we haven't looked," said Rose. "The attic!"

"That must be where he is," said Father. "I went up there to get a box this morning, and he must have come up without my noticing."

So the attic stairs were pulled down again. Ulysses didn't need to be called. He was right there, waiting, and came down almost as soon as the stairs did. He had finished his nap long ago, and he was very lonely, and nearly starved besides. But he never liked to mew.

"Poor cat!" said Rose, patting him, while he rubbed up against her legs and began to purr.

"Never mind, Ulysses, your dinner is all ready for you," said Judith.

"Our dinner is all ready, too," said Mother.

So the family sat down to eat their dinner while it was still hot, and Ulysses ran to the kitchen to eat his dinner. He ate up all the cat food and almost ate the plate! But when his meal was finished and he was ready to rest again, Ulysses pattered up the stairs and sat in the hall, looking up at the trap door.

Even though he had been shut up in the attic for three hours, he wanted to go there again. The doll's cradle was a very comfortable bed!

When the table was set, and before the family had come into the dining room, Ulysses would jump up on a chair.

5

THE TWO PINCUSHIONS

ALTHOUGH he was a full-grown cat, Ulysses liked to play. Judith and Rose played with him often when they weren't at school or out of doors. They fastened spools to the ends of strings and dragged them across the floor for Ulysses to chase. And they tied spools to the banisters too, for Ulysses to bat back and forth.

Ulysses liked to play with spools, but he liked to play with napkins even better! Playing with napkins was not allowed. Perhaps that was why.

When the table was set, and before the family had come into the dining room, Ulysses would jump up on a chair. His round green eyes could just see over the edge of the table. He would seize the nearest napkin with one claw and roll it on to the floor, ring and all. Then down he'd jump and begin chasing it. He could never chase it very far, though, because someone always heard him and took the napkin away from him and shooed him out of the dining–room.

One day Ulysses was wandering around the house, looking for something to do. He had been out of doors in the fresh air for a long time and was feeling frisky. He heard voices in the living room, so he went in there.

Mother was sewing, with her workbasket beside her. Rose and Judith were sewing too, making clothes for their Teddy bears.

Ulysses jumped on the couch beside Mother and then jumped down again.

"Oh, look!" cried Rose. "Ulysses has your pincushion!"

Ulysses had the pincushion between his paws. He tossed it up in the air and when it fell to the floor all the pins in it made a lovely rattling sound. Ulysses pounced on the pincushion as though it were a mouse, but just then Judith rescued it and gave it back to Mother.

Ulysses walked out of the room with his ears back.

But the next day he took the pincushion out of the basket again. He batted it around the floor for some time before he was dis-covered and the pincushion was taken away from him.

"Let's make him one of his own," said Rose.

"That's a good idea," said Mother. "Then he won't keep taking mine."

So Judith made a little square pin-cushion, just exactly like Mother's. Rose put the stuffing in it, and Mother put some pins in, so that it would make the same sound that hers did when it was pushed along the floor. She put only safety-pins in it, though, so that Ulysses wouldn't get his paws pricked.

When the new pincushion was finished it was tossed on the floor, right in front of Ulysses. He had watched it being made with great interest, and he was waiting for it. He sniffed at it, and then he batted it with one paw. But he didn't play with it long. Even though he knew it had been very kind of Rose and Judith to make it for him, he didn't like it quite as well as the other one for some reason. He soon left it lying behind a radiator.

A little later, when Mother looked in her work-basket, she saw that her own pin-cushion had disappeared again!

Of course she knew what had happened. She went to look for Ulysses, and found him lying asleep in a corner of the dining room. Beside him was her pincushion, looking somewhat chewed.

"Ulysses!" said Mother.

Ulysses opened one eye.

"What shall I do?" said Mother.

She took the pincushion and went up-stairs, thinking all the while. She remembered the napkins and how much Ulysses liked to play with them, and she thought she knew why he liked her pincushion better than his own. He was not allowed to play with it!

So Mother had a very good idea, and this is what she did. She put her own pincushion in one of the bureau drawers where it was safely hidden, and she put Ulysses' pincushion in her work-basket. Then she and Judith and Rose all waited to see what would happen.

Ulysses batted the pincushion out of the basket.

They didn't have to wait very long. While they were pretending not to look, they watched Ulysses come into the room.

Quickly and carefully he hooked the pincushion out of the basket and batted it around happily, feeling as though he were doing something he wasn't allowed to do.

And he didn't know that he was playing with his own pincushion all the time!

Maybe he found out, later, because he was a clever cat. But probably by that time he wasn't interested in pincushions at all any more.

Ulysses was not interested in playing with his *own* pincushion.

The Clever Cat

6

THE CATNIP MOUSE

THE snow began to melt in the spring. It took a long time for it to melt, because there was so much of it. First it turned into slush, and then the slush turned into mud. Judith and Rose liked to put on high rubber boots and go out wading in the mud. Jimmy, the little boy next door, had high rubber boots too, and he played out of doors with Rose and Judith and helped them find new puddles to wade in.

Ulysses didn't like the mud any better than the snow. He didn't have any rubber boots. When he went outdoors he walked very carefully, stepping high. The only times he ran were when Blackie chased him, or when he chased Blackie.

Mother thought that Ulysses ought to have a tonic in the spring, so she bought him some catnip. Of course Ulysses loved catnip. Most cats do. It was good for him, too, just as good as cod-liver oil is for children, and much nicer.

The first time Mother gave Ulysses some catnip she put it on a plate under the kitchen table, where it looked neat and was out of the way. But Ulysses was so excited by the catnip that he wouldn't eat it off a plate the way he did his other food. He scattered it all over the floor and rolled in it. So the next time Mother gave him some catnip she didn't put it on a plate. She put it in a little pile instead, under the kitchen table.

One day Mother took Judith and Rose shopping with her. They went to the Five and Ten. Judith and Rose each had a purse, and in their purses was some money. They had been saving their allowances. They bought some blankets for their dolls and some ear-rings for their toy kangaroos and some post-cards to send to their relations. And then, just after they had spent all their money, they saw some catnip mice!

"Oh!" said Rose. "There is something that Ulysses would like!"

"But we haven't any money left," said Judith sadly.

"Never mind," said Mother. "I will buy a catnip mouse and you may give it to Ulysses as a present from all of us."

Mother bought the catnip mouse, and Judith and Rose could hardly wait to take it home and show it to Ulysses. And when Ulysses saw it he was so excited that he hardly knew what to do. He ran around in circles, and he sniffed at the mouse, and chewed it. He tossed it in the air and caught it again, and danced on his hind legs! The family all gathered around to watch him, and laughed and laughed. The catnip mouse was almost as much fun for everyone else as it was for Ulysses.

Every day Ulysses played with his catnip mouse, until after a while it really didn't look much like a mouse any more.

Every day Ulysses played with his mouse, until after a while it really didn't look much like a mouse any more. Its tail was gone and it didn't have any ears. Whenever Ulysses grew tired of playing with it he went off to rest somewhere. Then the mouse was usually found lying in some strange place.

Sometimes it was under a radiator, sometimes behind a door. Sometimes it was on a bed, and once it was in a waste-paper basket, and nearly was thrown away by mistake.

But once it seemed to be lost, and no one saw it for a long, long time. Finally it was discovered in the strangest place of all. It was under the kitchen table, right in the middle of a fresh pile of catnip!

There was only one reason for Ulysses leaving it there, as Father pointed out to the children. The catnip mouse had lost its flavor, and so Ulysses had laid it on the fresh catnip pile to make it taste good again.

"He certainly is a clever cat!" said everyone.

Ulysses came into the kitchen, waving his tail. He didn't say anything, but he looked more important than ever, and purred and purred!

7

ULYSSES GOES HUNTING

BY THE time the mud had disappeared the grass had begun to grow, and it really looked like spring. There were buds on the lilac bushes around the house, and the willow trees that were between the garden and the meadow had gold-colored branches. Soon there would be leaves on them. Beyond the meadow the hills were turning green. It was lovely out of doors.

The children played in the garden all the time when they were not in school, and even Ulysses liked to be in the garden better than in the house now. He liked to sharpen his claws on the tree trunks and play hide and seek with Judith and Rose around the bushes. But the thing that he liked best to do was to watch the robins.

The robins had come on the first warm day, and they were very busy in the garden hunting for fat juicy worms and looking for good places to build their nests in.

The robins didn't seem to be afraid of anything, not even a big black cat. They hopped saucily across the lawn where the new grass was growing, puffing out their red breasts and acting as though the garden belonged to them.

Ulysses liked to sharpen his claws on the tree trunks.

One day the whole family was out in the garden. Father and Mother were talking around the house looking at the lilac bushes, Judith and Rose were with them, asking questions and wanting to know how soon there would be flowers. Ulysses followed behind. He liked to be with the family, but every once in a while he stopped to look at a robin.

There was one robin bigger than all the rest. He hopped across the lawn and came right towards Ulysses. His tail feathers stood up behind, and his head was cocked on one side. His red breast looked very proud.

Nearer and nearer he came, and Ulysses crouched down. His round green eyes glared at the robin, but the robin wasn't afraid. He hopped one hop nearer. Up jumped Ulysses, with one paw stretched out. He wanted to catch the saucy robin. But even though he was quick, the robin was quicker. He flew away just in time, and perched on the highest branch of the tallest poplar tree. Ulysses sat down with his ears back.

Soon another robin came hopping along. Ulysses crouched down again. He hunched himself into a ball and twitched the tip of his tail. But this robin was not as brave as the first one. Before Ulysses had time to spring the robin saw him and flew away. He perched up in the top of a tree, higher than a cat could climb. Ulysses walked away, pretending that he wasn't interested in robins any more.

But the next time he saw a robin, he was just as interested as ever.

Judith and Rose didn't like to see Ulysses chasing robins. They were afraid that he might catch one sometime.

"What would he do if he caught one?" asked Rose. "Would he eat it?"

"I don't see why he should want to eat robins," said Judith. "He always has so much cat food and salmon and things to eat!"

"Just the same, I hope he doesn't catch any robins," said Rose.

"So do I," said Judith. "Poor robins!"

"I don't think Ulysses will ever catch a robin, children," said Mother. "He is not quite quick enough. Besides, he is so big and black that they can see him a long way off."

"Sh-sh," said Father. "Don't speak so loudly. You might hurt Ulysses' feelings."

Ulysses was not far away, and he had sharp ears. Maybe he heard what Mother said. At any rate, after that he seemed to try harder than ever to catch a robin. Every day he went hunting, and spent long hours crouching in the grass, or sitting under trees waiting for the robins to come down and look for worms. Day after day he hunted, but he must have been either too slow, or too big and black. He didn't catch a robin.

The family all decided that if Ulysses ever *should* catch one, it would surprise him very much.

Every day Ulysses went hunting.

But one day it was everyone else who was surprised. While the family were in the dining room having dinner they suddenly heard a flapping, twittering sound on the back porch, and then a bumping sound against the back door. They all hurried to the back porch to see what was happening.

There on the back porch stood Ulysses. His eyes were as bright as electric lights and his whiskers were more excited looking than they had ever been before. For there is his mouth was a robin!

"Oh! Oh!" cried Judith and Rose, jumping up and down.

But as soon as Ulysses saw all the family in the doorway he let go of the robin. It wasn't hurt at all. It flew away quickly without once looking back.

"He didn't kill it," said Rose.

"No," said Father. "I think he only wanted to show us that he *could* catch a robin. That's why he brought it to the back door."

Ulysses rubbed up against Father's legs, and then walked into the kitchen, where a nice dish of salmon was waiting for him under the table. He looked up just once, and that was because he wanted to say, "*This* is what cats like to eat, not birds!"

Ulysses looked up just once as if he wanted to say, "*This* is what cats like to eat, not birds!"

The Clever Cat

8

THE BLACK PANTHER
AND THE SEA LION

IN THE summer Ulysses liked to be out of doors so much that he didn't want to come in at night. He thought it was more fun to spend the night in the garden than in the cellar. He didn't mind not having his wheelbarrow bed out of doors, because he didn't care to go to sleep at night in the summer. There were too many crickets and field mice and robins around.

Father was usually the first one of the family to get up in the morning, because he had to go downstairs to look at the hot water heater. When he went downstairs he opened the back door and called Ulysses. Ulysses was always glad to come into the house again by the time it was morning, and he was always hungry too. But he would never eat any breakfast until after Father had picked him up and patted him.

As soon as he had finished his breakfast Ulysses always ran upstairs to see how Mother and Judith and Rose were. He jumped on their beds, and sometimes patted them gently on their cheeks with his paw.

Ulysses would have had a very peaceful time if it hadn't been for Blackie. He and Blackie were still enemies. Whenever they saw each other they fought, and so there were many cat fights. Sometimes the fights were tree fights and sometimes they were back-door-fights.

When a fight was a tree fight it ended with either Blackie or Ulysses, or both, in a tree. When it was a back-door-fight it ended with each cat at his own back door, asking to be let in. Ulysses often came home with a chewed ear, and once he came home with a rather chewed-looking spot at the end of his tail.

"I wish those two cats wouldn't fight all the time," said Judith.

"So do I," said Rose.

"Cats aren't as nice as dogs, anyway," said Jimmy. "I'm going to have a dog for my birthday."

Ulysses didn't know much about dogs, yet. But he had heard of black panthers. In the middle of the summer, when the corn grew tall at the foot of the vegetable garden, he liked to walk up and down between the rows of corn. Then Judith and Rose would say, "He looks just like a black panther in the jungle."

Ulysses liked being a black panther. Down in the corn jungle there was no other animal except himself.

One day Ulysses was having a nap in the jungle. It was a hot day, and quiet. The only sound in the garden was the noise the bees made buzzing around the flower beds.

Ulysses liked being a black panther in the corn jungle.

Father was peacefully weeding the lawn, and Mother was sitting in a chair near by reading. Judith and Rose had gone to play with some friends.

"How quiet it is," said Mother.

Just then there came the sound of running feet, and around the corner of the house came Judith and Rose, with six friends. They all had on either bathing suits or sun suits, and they all cried out at once, "We want to be hosed! We want to be hosed!"

"Please, Father, won't you turn on the hose?" said Judith.

"We're almost roasting!" said Rose. "It's so hot."

Father decided that there might as well be a hosing party, so he stopped weeding the lawn and went to get the long garden hose. He fastened it to the water spigot that was at the side of the house, and turned the handle of the spigot. The water came out with a rush, and sprayed like a huge fountain across the lawn. The children began to squeal.

"Now," said Father, "who wants to have the first turn?"

All the children cried out at once, "I do! I do!"

They shrieked, and jumped up and down, and one by one they ran under the shower of water, crying, "Oh! It's cold!" and "My turn next!"

The noise the children made woke up Ulysses. It was louder than a cat fight, he thought. Without even waiting to stretch himself the black panther came trotting out of the jungle, eager to see what was happening on the lawn.

The children ran back and forth through the shower as Ulysses watched.

There were all the children running through the spray, and the sun shone on the water and made a rainbow in it. Ulysses came nearer.

"Look out, the cat will get wet!" cried one child.

"Oh, Ulysses, don't get so close," said Rose.

But Ulysses was not afraid of the water. It looked like something to play with. He put out one paw, and some drops sprinkled on it. And at that moment a little boy who had run around behind Father, jiggled his arm. The hose made a sudden jerk, and the water went all over Ulysses.

Father turned the hose in another direction right away, but it was too late. Ulysses was wet from the tips of his ears to the tip of his tail.

Poor Ulysses! He found out that he didn't like water, after all. He shook himself, and coughed. His fur was as wet and shining as a sea lion's, and he looked far more like a sea lion than a black panther.

The children ran to pat him, and Mother said, "Come here, Ulysses, and lie down in the sun."

"He'll soon dry off in the sun," said Father.

But Ulysses walked away. Back to his jungle he went, slowly and sadly, shaking drops of water off his whiskers. It was far more fun being a black panther than a sea lion.

9

TRAINING A CAT

THERE were some kinds of food that Ulysses didn't like to eat at all, and there were other kinds of food that he liked very much. He was especially fond of fish, and hamburger, and cat food, and there were a few vegetables that he liked too. His favorite vegetable was asparagus. He purred when he ate it.

Judith was reading an exciting book one day. It was by a man who trained wild lions and tigers for the circus, and it told about how he taught them to do tricks. The first thing he taught a wild lion or tiger to do was to climb up on a stool when he was told to.

"That sounds easy," thought Judith. She closed the book, because she had had an idea. If this man could teach lions and tigers tricks, maybe she could teach Ulysses a few tricks. He was very clever. He was certainly as clever as a lion or a tiger. What fun it would be to have a trained cat!

Judith told Rose her idea, and Rose thought it was a good one. "Where is Ulysses?" she said.

"Somewhere around," said Judith. "You go and look for him, and I'll find a stool, and then we can begin teaching him tricks."

Judith thought she could teach Ulysses to climb up on a stool.

So Rose ran off to hunt for Ulysses, and Judith went into the kitchen to get the kitchen stool. It was a high wooden one, painted blue. Judith carried it out of doors and set it up on the lawn. Then she found a stick. Trainers always held sticks when they were training animals. They used them to point with, to show the animals what they were meant to do.

Meanwhile Rose found Ulysses. He was down at the edge of the meadow, chasing grasshoppers. She carried him over to the stool and put him down in front of it. Ulysses seemed rather surprised. He was probably wondering what the kitchen stool was doing out on the lawn.

Judith tapped the top of the stool with her stick.

"Jump up, Ulysses," she said.

Ulysses thought she was playing with him. He stood up on his hind legs and batted the stick. But he didn't jump up on the stool.

Rose patted the top of the stool with her hands. "Come on, jump up," she said.

Ulysses thought that Rose was playing with him, too. He pounced at her fingers, but still he didn't jump up on the stool.

"We'll have to start all over again," said Judith.

She made Ulysses sit down on the grass, a little way off. Then she pointed at him with the end of her stick, and then pointed at the stool. "Jump up!" she said.
But Ulysses had seen a grasshopper. He pounced at it instead of jumping on the stool. The grasshopper hopped away, and Ulysses pounced again.

"Oh, dear!" said Judith. "What shall we do?"

"He's not a bit interested in the stool," said Rose.

"I know what let's do," said Judith. "Let's put something that he likes on top of the stool. Then maybe he'll jump up. Can you think of anything he especially likes?"

"Oh, yes!" said Rose, "Let's put something to eat up there." Rose ran into the kitchen and looked in the refrigerator. There was some cold left-over asparagus. It was just the thing.

"Mother, may I have one piece of asparagus?" Rose called.

"Yes," said Mother.

"We're teaching Ulysses tricks," said Rose. "Please come out and see!"

She hurried out of doors with the asparagus, and there was Judith, holding Ulysses so that he couldn't run away. Rose laid the piece of asparagus on top of the stool. It looked very delicious.

"Oh," said Judith. "Asparagus! Now let's see what Ulysses will do."

Ulysses was already scrambling out of her arms. His nose was wrinkling and his eyes were popping. He stood up on his hind legs with his paws on the edge of the stool, and sniffed at the asparagus.

"What if he eats it before he jumps up!" said Rose.

Judith picked up the piece of asparagus before Ulysses had time to eat it. She held it in the air, a little way above the stool.

"Now jump up," she said. "Come, Ulysses!"

And this time Ulysses did jump up, just as he was told to. There he sat on the kitchen stool, like one of the lions and tigers in the book. His head was lifted towards the asparagus, and Judith, as a prize, gave it to him to eat.

Ulysses sat on the kitchen stool, like one of the lions and tigers in the book.

When Mother came out to see whether Ulysses had learned any tricks yet or not, she saw him sitting on the stool, looking very pleased and proud.

"We've taught Ulysses his first trick," said Judith and Rose. "He jumped up on the stool when we told him to."

The trained cat purred and purred. He had just finished eating the asparagus, and it was very good.

10

ROWDY, THE DOG

AFTER Ulysses had learned one trick it was not so hard for him to learn others. Father taught him a trick, too. When Father said, "Flap your tail, Ulysses," Ulysses flapped his tail. Sometimes he flapped his whole tail and sometimes he flapped just the tip of it. Ulysses liked to do this trick best lying down. It was hard for him to do it right when he was standing up.

Once Ulysses heard a visitor say, "Why, he wages his tail just like a dog, doesn't he?" But Ulysses didn't like that. He didn't wag his tail like a dog. He f*lapped* it, like a cat. And he wondered why people kept talking about dogs, anyway.

At the end of the summer Jimmy, the little boy next door, had a birthday. He was six years old. His mother gave a big party for him, and invited all his friends. Judith and Rose were invited. They hadn't been to a birthday party for quite a long time, and they were very much excited. They wore their best dresses, and ribbons on their hair.

Judith and Rose each took Jimmy a present. Judith gave him a book about Indians, and Rose gave him a lavender Teddy bear that she almost wished she could have kept for herself.

It was a lovely birthday party. The children all played games on the lawn, and afterwards they had ice cream and cake to eat, and fancy paper hats to wear, and favors. Some of the favors were whistles. The children were having a very good time, judging by the noise. Ulysses sat on the doorstep, listening.

He heard the sound of children playing, and the sound of children laughing, and the sound of children blowing whistles. And then all at once he heard another sound, mixed with these. It was such an awful sound that it made the fur on his back bristle. It was a bark!

Ulysses stood up and arched his back, while his tail grew bigger and bigger. The barking noise came nearer.

Ulysses couldn't see the birthday party, even though he could hear It., because there were high bushes between him and the lawn next door where the party was. But suddenly through the bushes there came bounding a strange animal. It was brown and white animal, with a collar around its neck, and a short wagging tail. It was a dog.

"Wow! Wow!" said the dog, standing still.

Ulysses didn't say anything, but he arched his back still higher, and made himself all ready to spring in case the dog should come any nearer. This was another enemy, he thought, a worse enemy than Blackie.

"Woof," said the dog, with his head on one side, and his tail still wagging. He came one step nearer.

Ulysses stepped back. And the next minute he would probably have jumped at the dog, if Jimmy hadn't called just then, "Here, Rowdy! Here, Rowdy!"

"Woof", said the dog again. He turned his back on Ulysses and bounded away through the bushes. Ulysses didn't follow him. Instead, he went around to the back door, which was open, and when he was in the house he felt much happier. He wished that there were no such things as dogs.

Judith and Rose came home from the party, talking excitedly. They wanted to tell Father and Mother all about the party, and they both talked at the same time, which made it rather hard to understand what they were saying.

Ulysses was curled in an armchair. He didn't pay much attention until he heard the word, "dog."

Ulysses, who was curled up in an armchair, didn't pay much attention until he heard the word, "dog." Then he pricked up his ears.

"Jimmy's father and mother gave him a dog for a birthday present," Rose was saying.

"His name is Rowdy," said Judith.

"He is a Boston bull," said Rose.

"And he is very nice and friendly, and he comes when he is called," said Judith.

Ulysses stretched. "Friendly," he thought. "Well he didn't *sound* very friendly."

Father patted him. "I wonder how Ulysses will like having a dog next door," he said.

Ulysses knew, though he didn't say anything.

But when Mother said, "I think our cat is nicer than any dog," he flapped the tip of his tail without even being asked!

11

FRIENDS

ROWDY was really a very nice dog. He meant to be friendly, and the only reason he barked was because he was a dog, and felt that he had to say something. Rowdy wanted to play with Ulysses; but his bark was so loud, and his ways were so sudden, that whenever he came bounding across the lawn Ulysses always seemed to want to go in the opposite direction just as fast as he could.

One day Ulysses heard Rose say, "I just saw Rowdy chasing Blackie! He chased him up a tree, and then he barked at him. Blackie stayed up the tree until Rowdy had gone away."

Ulysses was interested. For the first time he began to feel as though some day he might begin to like Blackie. Blackie was not as noisy as Rowdy and he was much nicer looking, Ulysses thought.

The fall came early, and soon the days were cold again; and the nights were so cold that Ulysses slept in the cellar once more, curled up tightly in his wheelbarrow. The wind blew the leaves off the trees, and they lay along the paths and crackled when they were walked on. There wasn't any corn jungle any more, and there weren't any flowers, either.

School had begun again, so that Judith and Rose were away for most of the day. The house seemed quiet now, and a little lonely.

Ulysses spent most of his time indoors, just as he had in the winter. But Father put him out of doors for a while every day, as he needed the fresh air.

Ulysses didn't like to go very far away from the house and the family. When he was put outside he usually sat hunched up on the doorstep, looking very cold, and waiting to be let in. He would sit there, like a black ball, and think longingly of the fire in the fireplace, and of the red and gray rug in front of it.

One evening Father went to the door to call Ulysses. He had put him out some time ago, and he was afraid that he must be very cold by now. He expected to find Ulysses sitting as close to the door as he could get. But when he opened the door no cat came running in.

It was rather dark outside, so Father turned on the light above the door and looked again. And what he saw was a sight so strange that he could hardly believe his eyes. For there were *two* black cats on the doorstep.

Hunched up peacefully at one end was Ulysses. And hunched up peacefully at the other end was Blackie. Side by side they sat, like two lions guarding a building, and they looked as happy and contented as though they had been friends all their lives.

After all, they were both cats.

There were two black cats on the doorstep.

The Clever Cat

12

CHRISTMAS

JUDITH and Rose began to talk about Christmas long before it was time for Christmas. They each made a list of the presents they wanted, and then they each made a list of the presents they wanted to give other people.

"What are you going to give Ulysses, Rose?" asked Judith.

"I don't know, but I think I'll give him a hairbrush," said Rose. "He needs one very badly. What are you going to give him?"

At that moment Ulysses walked into the room, looking interested.

"Whisper it to me," said Rose.

Judith whispered something in Rose's ear, so that Ulysses couldn't hear.

"Oh," said Rose. "But he's had one of those before."

"I know," said Judith. "I'm sure he'd like another one, though."

Ulysses began to wash himself, and Judith and Rose went on talking. They were wondering how many of the presents on their lists they would get, and wishing that Christmas would hurry up and come, because they were tired of waiting for it.

The last two weeks before Christmas were exciting ones. The mailman kept bringing mysterious packages to the house that Rose and Judith were not allowed to open. Mother took all the packages upstairs to her room and hid them away in bureau drawers.

Then Rose and Judith went shopping and brought back little packages of their own, which they hid away in *their* bureau drawers. There were presents for Father and Mother, and for each other, and for their aunts and uncles who were coming to spend Christmas with them. There were also two presents for Ulysses.

The day before Christmas Father put holly-wreaths in all the downstairs windows. A truck drove up to the front door with a tall Christmas tree in it, and Father set the tree up at one end of the living room. Mother went up in the attic to fetch the Christmas tree trimmings that were kept there in a trunk. And Ulysses followed at her heels, as eager as ever to explore the attic.

When Mother came down from the attic she held two boxes of Christmas tree trimmings in her hands. Judith and Rose helped her trim the tree, and when it was all trimmed it looked lovely. There were shining colored balls on it, and silver snow, and tiny candles. On the very highest point there was a star.

Judith and Rose helped trim the Christmas tree.

Soon the uncles and aunts arrived, with more packages and many suitcases. The house was full of people, all talking and laughing.

As soon as it was dark Father lighted the candles on the tree. All the packages had been brought down from upstairs, and they were arranged in a huge pile on a table in the living room. There were packages of all sizes and shapes, tied with ribbons of all colors.

Judith and Rose walked round and round the table, wondering what was inside all the packages, and gently pinching the ones that were marked with their own names. They wished for the hundredth time that tomorrow would hurry up and come, because they were not supposed to open their presents until Christmas Day.

Suddenly Father said, "Where is Ulysses?"

"He ought to come in and see the tree," said Mother.

Judith and Rose ran to the door to call him. But no cat was there.

"Where can he be?" said Father. "I am sure he didn't go down into the cellar."

Then Mother said, "I wonder if he could have been shut up in the attic again? I remember his following me up there today, but I can't remember whether he came down with me or not."

I'll go and see," said Father.

Father went upstairs and opened the trap door. Down slid the attic stairs, and on the top step there was standing a big black cat with round owl-like eyes! Poor Ulysses had been shut up in the attic all afternoon.

"Poor Ulysses!" said Mother and Rose and Judith when Father brought him into the living room. They felt sorry that they hadn't missed him sooner. They had all been so busy that they had forgotten they had a cat.

"What a handsome cat he is!" said one of the uncles.

"Would he stay in my lap if I picked him up?" asked one of the aunts.

But Ulysses had seen the table with all the presents on it. Without even waiting to be patted, he walked across the room and jumped up on the table. Quick as a flash he jumped down again, but one claw of his right paw was hooked through the ribbon of a small parcel. On the tag was printed, "ULYSSES," in large clear letters. It was his own present that he had picked out, as everyone could see.

"Ulysses can read!" cried Rose.

"He certainly *seems* to be able to," said Mother. "Shall we give him his present now, since he has already picked it out?"

"Oh, yes!" said Judith. "And I'll unwrap it for him, because it's the present I gave him."

So Judith unhooked the small parcel from Ulysses' claw, and unwrapped it. A catnip mouse was inside!

61

Ulysses did not wait to be patted. He walked across the room and jumped up on the table.

Christmas Day was a happy day for Judith and Rose. They were given almost all the things that were on their lists, and other things that weren't on their lists, but that they liked too. Christmas Day was also a happy day for Ulysses. He had a catnip mouse and a hairbrush, and a little red ball, and a new saucer to drink out of.

No one knew whether Ulysses could really read his own name, or whether the reason he picked out his own present was because he smelled the catnip mouse inside. No one knew. But whichever it was, everyone agreed that he was certainly a very clever cat.

And as there really is a cat named Ulysses, living in a white house in New Hampshire, there is no way of telling how many more clever things he may do yet.

THE END

The Clever Cat

About the Author

Eleanor Frances Lattimore was born in China where her father and mother had gone to teach English at a Chinese government university. Eleanor was the fourth of five children. She had two older sisters, Katharine and Isabel, an older brother Owen, and a younger brother Richmond, whom the family called Dick.

Eleanor was especially close to her sister, Isabel, who was only two years older. From the time Eleanor was four or five years old, she and Isabel cut out paper dolls, colored them, gave the paper dolls names, and wrote stories about them. They collected these stories in little home-made books. Both girls were sure, even then, that they wanted to be artists when they grew up.

The Lattimore children were taught by their parents. They were "home-schooled", although that term was not used then. Owen was sent to public school in England in 1912, when he was 12.

The Lattimore family returned to the United States in 1920, when Isabel was 18 and Eleanor 16. Isabel and Eleanor studied art in Oakland, California, for a year before joining their parents and Dick in Hanover, New Hampshire, where their father was now teaching at Dartmouth College.

Owen had finished school in England and returned to China where he was working for a large insurance company. Katharine was working in New York City as a secretary.

Isabel married first and soon had two little girls of her own, Marguerite and Audrey. Later, she had a boy, David, and another girl, Marisa. Isabel was an artist and also wrote poetry. (Eleanor always said Isabel was a better artist than she was.)

Eleanor studied art in New York City and Boston and worked for several years in New York City as a freelance artist, designing greeting cards and Christmas cards and illustrating books for children.

One day Eleanor went to see a children's book editor to see if she had any work for her to do. The editor, Elizabeth Bevier, especially liked Eleanor's drawings of little Chinese children. "It's too bad we don't have a book about a little Chinese child," said Miss Bevier, "because if we did I'd want you to make the illustrations for it."

Eleanor took this as an invitation for her to write a book! So she went back to her apartment and in about a week she wrote a book about a mischievous little Chinese boy named "Little Pear." Katharine typed the book for her on her typewriter. When she had finished, Eleanor took the manuscript to Miss Bevier. "Here is what I've written," she said.

"Well, I'll certainly take a look at it," said Miss Bevier, adding, "I'll call you when I've read it."

When Miss Bevier had read it, she phoned Eleanor and said, "We love it! We'll publish it as soon as you finish the illustrations." Miss Bevier said that because, of course, she wanted Eleanor to illustrate the book. *Little Pear* was published in 1931 and it is still in print, 84 years later.

Altogether, Eleanor published 57 books between 1931 and 1978. There were three more books about Little Pear – *Little Pear and his Friends* (1934), *Little Pear and the Rabbits* (1956) and *More About Little Pear* (1971).

Most of Eleanor's books are written for children in second and third grade. They are written simply and directly and are about things that happen in everyday life: falling in the water, losing a key and getting it back, getting to know a cousin from another part of the country, and so on.

Many of Eleanor's books are set in China where she grew up. Others are set in places where she lived. Many of her books are loosely based on the adventures of her children and grandchildren.

The Clever Cat (1936) is based on the adventures of a real cat named Ulysses who belonged to Eleanor's father. Judith and Rose were really Isabel's daughters, Marguerite and Audrey.

Made in the USA
Charleston, SC
04 March 2016